A FLING FOR CHRISTMAS

IRIS WEST

To you, my reader. I hope you love Blossom Ford, and the sexy men, curvy women and kind but extremely interfering folk that live there, as much as I do.

CHAPTER ONE

Aiyana

IT'S ONLY THE second day of December, but Blossom Ford is already in full Christmas mode. A popular version of Jingle Bells blares out of the speakers at the bar. Sprigs of mistletoe hang from strategic places and bright colored tinsel is draped over every single chair. It's a waste of labor and money. Honestly, if it weren't for Carmen, I wouldn't be here.

"One day you're going to fall in love with Christmas, querida," she says, shaking her head of dark curls. Spanish words tumble out of her, as they often do when she's tipsy.

"It hasn't happened in the last twenty-five years. I can't see it happening now."

I don't dislike all the festivities, it's just a little hard seeing everyone get together with their loved ones. I'm extremely lucky to have my four besties, who are practically family. And I'm no longer that little girl who used to cry because she wanted a mom, dad, hell, even a granny like Carmen had, to wave to her during the nativity play.

"You just need to fall in love and have a few babies. Making the holidays special for them will help you love it."

"I tried enough. Being dumped by four serious boyfriends in the space of seven years is enough. I told you, I'm not cut out for relationships."

Carmen shakes her head again. I don't know if it's because her granny brought her up, but she's always seemed wise beyond her years. "You wanted those relationships to be serious. You even believed they were. Everyone of your boyfriends was crazy for you, but you were always afraid to give all of yourself to them, in case you did and they abandoned you. Maybe, for the right man, you'll find the courage."

"Whatever. There's no point in trying again, is there?"

"Are you serious about having a temporary fling?"

I'm glad she dropped the boyfriend conversation. But now I'm wishing I never mentioned having a casual relationship. It was something I said offhandedly one day at my place, when we were having a rare girls' night.

"Why not? I worked hard to become a resident vet at my favorite zoo and get my apartment. I feel settled at work now and have more time."

"You could have twice, maybe three times, your salary if you accepted one of the jobs in those fancy city zoos."

"You know how we dreamed of leaving town when we were kids?" Carmen nods. "After my long college years and internship in California, I knew I wanted to settle here."

"Okay. You deserve a fling for Christmas." She giggles, then hiccups.

I laugh with her.

It's been over eighteen months since I got laid. There's only so much a battery-operated boyfriend can do. Since I'm no longer going to date, a fling is the next thing, or should I be saying a sexual partner? There must be a name for those kinds of things. I've always thought of myself as quite experienced in all things bedroom related, but I guess I'm not. I've only done it with my boyfriends. Never had a one-night stand.

"You need the right man." Carmen places her wineglass on the table and stares around the crowded bar. She tucks her hands under her chin and stares fixedly behind me.

"What is it?" I ask, turning.

She sighs dreamily and pushes her glasses up her nose.

"Seriously, who are you drooling over?"

Other women are staring too. I crane my neck until I spot what, or rather, who, is grabbing their attention.

My heart stutters.

"That's Isabella's future brother-in-law, isn't it? Finn, the hockey player. Maybe those are his teammates? I bet when they are playing, the rink doesn't fill up just because they are the best in the National Hockey League. They are excellent eye candy."

"I think they are." I know damn well they are Finn's teammates because I recognize them. Since our friend Isabella's engagement party, when I met Finn for the first time, I've been watching hockey now and then. I've been thinking about his killer smile and the phoenix tattoo on his arm. It's the most beautiful ink art I've ever seen.

"What about Finn? For your fling?"

I almost spit beer out.

Carmen's eyebrows rise above her glasses.

"He's one of the hottest guys on the planet. According to a zookeeper who keeps up with the tabloids," I feel compelled to add.

"So? It's not like you to put yourself down."

"I'm not." I've more than accepted my plus sized body. Having curvy friends like Carmen and Isabella helped a lot.

"I saw the way you two looked at each other at the party."

There was interest in Finn's eyes the times we locked eyes, yet he flew out of town the next day and I went back to my busy life.

We finish our drinks and get ready to leave. I avoid bumping into people as I walk Carmen out. I can't help checking out Finn's table, but he's not there. A cab comes in our direction, and I quickly hail it down. It isn't easy getting a cab at this time of the night in Blossom Ford.

I wave Carmen off, then head back into the bar. I'm so desperate for the bathroom, I know I won't make it home if I don't go now.

Finn is absent, and his friends are putting their coats on. Disappointment runs through me, but I swallow it. If it's not meant to be, I will not fuss over it.

There's a massive line outside the women's restrooms. The men's side is clear. I stop myself groaning. I've complained about this many times. To me, it makes sense to make the men's smaller and enlarge the women's. But the management has done nothing about it.

I eye the men's restrooms again. There's no sound coming from inside. And no one is going in. I march toward the door, push it and come face to face with Finn.

I go hot all over.

He steps aside. The click clack of my boot heels is loud as I walk past. He exits the room, leaving me both relieved and a little peeved. Is he being a gentleman by letting me use the facilities quickly before anyone comes, or does he not remember me?

I use one cubicle in record time. I've used the men's

toilets before. It makes little sense to wait so long when there are available toilets, but some men think a woman is loose and up for anything if they find her using their space. Also, it doesn't smell as nice as the women's.

I open the door and Finn stares at me. "Hurry," he says, then grabs my hand.

Startled, I follow him past three burly men. Finn must be about six feet three. They are taller and heavier and look like they are spoiling for a fight.

Outside, Finn stops but looks back towards the bar door.

"Did you stop them from coming into the toilet?" My gaze follows his.

"No man was going in while you were inside."

My lips curl up. Warmth spreads through me.

"That's a nice thing to do for a stranger."

"You're not a stranger, are you, Aiyana?"

He remembers me. At least he remembers my name. He was being a gentleman in the bathroom, looking out for me.

"Hi Finn. Thanks for the kind gesture." He's just as handsome as I remember. Fair red hair, sea-green eyes and a lean yet muscular frame make my mouth water.

He smiles straight into my eyes. "I had an ulterior motive."

Does he know how much that smile is affecting me right now?

"What is it?"

"If you're walking home alone, let me accompany you. I'll wait until you and your friend, I think it's Carmen, are ready."

A thrill thrums through me as I realize he was aware of my presence. "Carmen left. I'm ready to go. What about your friends?"

"They left too."

I glance at the moon, the streetlights and the Christmas decorations around the bar and the shops down Maine street. Suddenly, the bright lights and colors in town don't make feel so lonely anymore.

Even if I hadn't planned to walk home, I would. I'm not passing up the opportunity to be in the company of the first man I'm attracted to after eighteen months.

CHAPTER TWO

Finn

I HAVE TOO much going on right now to be thinking about Aiyana Ford. My dream of being one of the best players in the NHL, which I lived for twenty years, is over. I have to decide what I'm going to do from here on, but for the first time in my life, I can't figure it out. All I've ever wanted to do since I was little is play hockey.

It's nice of my teammates to drop in like they did tonight for a round or two of beer on their way north after a match in nearby Garnet City. It's just drinking with them reminds me of my playing days and makes me want to be back in the rink with a stick in my hands.

I'm forty-one, so I know my career was ending soon.

Everyone said it was better to leave while I was still the best in the game, too. Still, I hoped I had another couple of years in me. Even though injury was a career hazard, and I had my fair share of minor ones, I prayed I'd never have one fatal to my career.

I breathe in the fresh, cold air and feel the pain in my chest ease up a little. When I gaze at Aiyana's face, it almost disappears. She's staring at the moon in wonder, her face upturned.

She fascinates me. Something about her makes me curious. The moment Isabella introduced us, I was attracted to her. She had the warmest brown eyes I'd ever seen and curves I wanted wrapped around my body. Her lips were the reddish purple of my favorite wine.

But I was only in Blossom Ford for a day. Besides, she was Isabella's friend. And I don't do serious relationships. Despite the interest in Aiyana's eyes, I wasn't sure she'd be interested in a casual relationship. So I left town, thinking I'd forget about her, like the many stunning women I've forgotten over the years.

Those warm brown eyes refused to leave my memory. Now and then, when I spoke with anyone from home, I'd remember them and wonder how she was doing. Hell, once I even asked Riordan to speak with Isabella just to ask how her friends were.

She's wearing a soft red coat. Denim hugs her shapely long legs. In her heeled boots, she's nearly six feet. The sudden sound of a Christmas song playing grabs my attention. A family is coming out of Jackson's Diner, the children chattering excitedly.

I don't realize I'm humming the song until Aiyana speaks.

"I can tell you love Christmas. Nice humming too."

She's looking at the reindeer on my sweater, visible through my open coat.

"It's my favorite time of the year. Don't you love it?"

"What do you love about it?"

Aiyana is staring at me like she really wants to know. Even with only the moonlight, Christmas and occasional overhead lights, I can see the puzzled expression in her eyes.

So I think about it before answering. She grew up at the orphanage. Not having had a home and a family of her own, she might not feel the same way about Christmas as I do.

"The excitement and warmth in the air. It makes me hope something nice is coming soon." I shrug. Aiyana is still looking at me, as if she's expecting more.

"Singing and decorating the Christmas tree. The jokes and teasing that inevitably happen when all my family is together, Mom and Aunt Caitlin's roast turkey," I say. "Don't you like the holidays?"

She looks away from me. "Not really. I enjoy getting presents though. Your mom's food is delicious too. I'm glad I'll get to eat plenty of it this Christmas. Isabella invited me and the girls. We're even sleeping over."

"Everyone will be stuffed or too drunk to drive

anywhere. That's Christmas at home. No one leaves until the food is finished, unless they will take on Mom and Aunt Caitlin."

Aiyana laughs. She looks so carefree. I want to see her smile like that more often.

"What would they do?"

"Volunteer us for Santa duty, church cleaning or worse."

Aiyana laughs again.

We cross a small street. She stops and gazes behind a dumpster.

"I have to check on a friend. It won't take long," she says.

A cat meows.

"Hi Cutie," Aiyana calls out softly and a straggly ginger tabby slinks towards us.

"Look what I've got you."

She removes a paper towel and small can of cat food out of her bag. Then she lays out the small feast.

The tabby approaches the food cautiously, all the time keeping its eyes on us. After sniffing for a bit, he devours the meal. Aiyana strokes its back and murmurs something I can't catch to it.

I want those hands on me, stroking just like that.

Am I seriously getting jealous of a cat? I shake my head. I've gone without too long. That must be why my body is on alert at the thought of Aiyana touching me.

The cat stretches, leaning into her caress.

I squat beside Aiyana and try to pet it too, but it

snarls and scampers away.

"Did I do something wrong? I rarely get that reaction from animals."

Aiyana shakes her head. She gathers the paper towel, empty can and throws them into the dumpster, then sanitizes her hands with gel she fishes out of her bag.

"I think his previous owner abused him. It took a couple months for him to allow me to pet him," she says as we resume walking.

"That's sad. It would have been nicer if he'd behaved like that because he was being jealous."

"What do you mean?"

The worry on her face is replaced by curiosity.

"He thought he was getting a beautiful woman all to himself and another man comes into the picture."

She chuckles and stops outside of a three-story building. "This is me,"

The place is well lit and looks safe.

I keep my hands in my pockets to stop myself from touching her.

"I want to kiss you," I say.

Her eyes widen.

"Honestly, I want to do a lot more."

She stares at me, hands inside her pockets too. "Why don't you?"

"I can't commit to anything. I might be in town for only a few day days until Christmas if I'm lucky."

"That's okay. I'm only looking for something casual. A few days or until Christmas."

My cock hardens. There's no way I can resist her.

CHAPTER THREE

Aiyana

I DON'T KNOW who reaches for whom first. As soon as we step into my apartment and I close the door, we're kissing. Long, drugging kisses that leave me gasping for air. It's just what I need.

I whimper into his mouth, and Finn squeezes my butt. His hands are all over my body, creating little sparks of fire on every part of me he can reach.

I take my coat off, wanting his hands on my bare skin. He does the same, his lips never leaving mine.

I'm so turned on just by kissing. Just when need more, Finn slides his hands inside my sweater. I'm expecting chilly hands, but his touch is warm. His hands glide up the bare skin on my sides and caress my breasts through the layer of my bra.

"I've been dying to touch you since I saw you across

the bar. You don't know how hard it was to resist the itch to ditch my friends and go over to your table. I didn't want to ruin your girl's night."

His hoarse voice makes me shiver.

I run my hands through his hair, stroking his scalp.

"That feels good," Finn whispers against the side of my mouth.

"I'm glad. Cause you're making me feel good all over."

The more we kiss, the more my panties get wet.

He squeezes my breast and rubs the nipples. The sensation of the silky material of my bra brushing against my sensitive skin makes me moan.

Finn catches the moan in his mouth, his delicious lips sucking my bottom one.

I rub myself against him. I can feel him even with both our jeans on.

He hisses. Pushes me back against the door.

"Aiyana."

His hand slips into my jeans and strokes me through my wet, silky underwear. I gyrate against his touch, needing more.

"You're dripping wet, baby."

He pushes the scrap of material on my bare mound aside and slips his fingers into my wet pussy.

I moan. I touch him, wanting him to feel some of the sweet torture he's putting me through.

He groans and bucks against my hand. Then turns me

so I'm facing the door.

Excitement rushes through me. I'm so ready; I'm about to beg Finn to fuck me.

He shoves my jeans down to my knees and gives my bottom a tap.

"Lean against the door."

His tone is hard. I love it. A shiver runs down my whole body. I press my palms against the door and bend forward until my head is almost touching the door. I feel exposed, leaning like this with my butt hanging in the air while Finn is fully clothed, but I'm thrilled too.

I turn my head so I can see him. He slips a condom on his large, jutting cock.

I spread my legs wider and push against him.

Finn grabs my hips and enters me in one go.

I moan at the delicious tightening sensation.

"Fuck Aiyana! You're so tight. You okay?"

I can hardly hear him, his usually lilting voice is so thick.

"God, Finn. Don't stop."

He fucks me. With long and powerful thrusts that stroke the tissues in my pussy just right.

He bends over me and flicks my clit.

I come. In a burst of sensation that has me shuddering in pleasure and leaves my limbs weak. Finn bucks behind me and groans.

I can't move so I stay where I am, hanging on to the door for support, enjoying the sound of our uneven breaths steady.

"Where's the light?"

"To your right."

He tries pressing the switch twice before light floods into the room. Then he pulls out of me and I hate how empty I feel.

But a moment later, his arms wrap around me and I'm alright again.

He turns me and kisses me slowly.

"I feel like a teenager." His sea-green eyes hold mine captive.

"I doubt you were this good in your teens."

He tucks a stray lock behind my ear. A smile plays along his lips. "I wasn't."

The ground tilts as Finn sweeps me off my feet, pants, boots and all. I squeak and hold on to his neck.

"Bedroom?"

I point, too surprised to speak. When I switch on the light in the bedroom, the sight of our half-naked bodies in the mirror cracks me up and I realize why it took Finn so long to walk to the bedroom. His jeans are halfway down his legs, hampering his movements.

His brows lift, and he switches his gaze from me to the mirror.

"Yeh, definitely inexperienced behavior. It's been a while. I'll have to show you my skills later."

There are two pink dots on his cheeks. He's embarrassed. Something moves in my chest, making it tight.

Finn's shoulders shake and the moment passes.

"It's been a while for me, too. I was satisfied, but if you want to do better, I'm up for it."

He nips my lip, drops me on the bed, removes his jeans and shorts then leaves the room. I watch him, eyes glued to his butt.

I'm not usually very shy about my body, but suddenly I get the jitters. Is being in a fling different from being in a steady relationship? I'm a hugger. Will he stay behind to cuddle and talk, or is he going to leave now that we've done it?

My eyes fall on his pants. Surely he would've kept them on if he was leaving.

I remove my clothes and put them on the chair under the window. I figure I might as well be comfortable and am getting under the quilt when Finn saunters back into the room.

He takes off his Christmas sweater, gets in beside me, he lies down on his back with his arms crossed under his head and stares at me.

"What?"

Although I'm tired, he's making me feel tingly all over.

"You're gorgeous."

That fuzzy feeling in my heart is back. Does he say this to all the women he sleeps with? The thought sneaks in. I brush it aside.

We're having a fling, I remind myself. Finn's gaze is clear. He looks like he meant the compliment but I should take it as a very sexy man complimenting a woman he finds attractive. I shouldn't be attaching any special meaning to it.

"So are you," I say lightly.

I lie down too.

"Wanna hug?" He asks.

I turn towards him. He snakes his arm under my head and tucks me closer to him. His arms travel up and down my back and butt.

I smile. I'm feeling so good right now, wrapped around his beautifully inked arms. Having a fling was the right thing to do.

I shove the warm fuzzy feeling away.

CHAPTER FOUR

Finn

I WAKE UP at the crack of dawn. Aiyana is sleeping in my arms, her shiny black locs spread over my chest. I stop myself from sliding my hands down her body and turning her so I can slip into her; then take my time loving her until she's making those moaning sounds that make me desire her more.

Carefully, I slide from under her body. I suck a breath in when her thigh bumps against my hard cock. I'm half hoping she'll wake up, but she carries on sleeping.

I'll be a dick if I wake her up.

I roll out of bed and get dressed as quietly as I can. In the living room, I switch on the light and search around for pen and paper. I leave a note, promising to get in touch later.

Then I exit her building and inhale the early morning winter air as I stride towards the bar. My truck is in the parking lot with other cars. I get in and head towards The Point. Excitement buzzes through me as I drive through the dark, empty streets.

I've been to The Point to watch the sunrise so many times, but this emotion of expectation never changes in intensity. Even when I was playing, and could make it home, watching the sunrise was one of the first things I always did.

It only takes a few minutes to get there. I park and get my torch. Out here, it's not as lit as the town.

I remove a blanket from the trunk and stride towards the ford and the cherry blossom tree that hangs over it. Its branches are almost bare but the old tree still looks stunning, lording over the still water. I veer off to the left and carry on walking. The path is so familiar, I can walk it with my eyes closed.

When the river turns, I cross the shrubbery to a clearing. It's the perfect spot. I've seen no one this far back. For the last ten years, I've heard someone nearby, but we've never crossed paths and that's how I like it.

It's half-past six. Usually, I'm here earlier.

I'm about to lay the blanket on the floor when I hear a sound. It's close. My sometimes neighbor must be coming. I spread the blanket on the floor and am about to sit down, so I can't be seen, when something red catches my attention.

It looks like the coat Aiyana was wearing yesterday.

Curious, I wait a little, thinking I have a bit more time to sit before she spots me. It's her. After last night, I'd know that easy stride of hers anywhere.

She suddenly stops. I was so stunned to see her here; I didn't sit when I should have. It's too late to pretend I didn't see her. And strangely, I don't want to.

"Aiyana. It's Finn."

Hugging a bright red blanket against her chest, she closes the short distance between us.

She shines a torch on my blanket, then points it downwards.

"Wanna sit together?" I'm not the only one surprised at my words.

Aiyana jerks her head toward her spot.

I wait, unsure why I asked the question. I protected my privacy for over twenty years. The only person who knows about this place is my twin, Rory. What's changed?

"You have the best spot. When I first started coming here, I was gutted it was taken."

"We can share it today."

She lays her blanket beside mine and sits with her legs crossed. I sit beside her.

After a while, the sun's first rays appear in the sky in hues of apricot and tangerine. The view is so amazing that for the first few moments, I can't take my eyes aways from it. I glance down at Aiyana and my breath hitches. She looks so beautiful. I can feel that her concentration is solely on the miracle unfolding in front of us.

I want to do this with her again. For a very long time.

I'm in love with her.

The fascination I've been feeling toward her, the odd behavior and how I was so excited to get inside her was all because of it.

At last, I've found the woman I want to spend the rest of my life with.

I know it deep in my heart.

I've enjoyed casual relationships with women all my adult life, but I've always hoped one day I'd find my soulmate like Mom and Dad. I never imagined it'd be at such a critical moment in my life. And with a woman I'm having a fling with to booth.

I face the sun again and watch the bright colors dance, humbled yet grateful. If a miracle like this can happen every day, I'm sure I'll decide my future and make Aiyana realize I'm the only man that can make her happy. I have to figure out why she's not doing relationships right now.

The peace around us settles me. We gaze at the sky silently, even as birds chirp and other sounds intrude on the quiet morning.

"Wow!" Aiyana whispers, almost to herself.

"When did you start coming? I noticed sounds from your spot around ten years ago."

She looks at me, as if she's wondering what to divulge.

"I was about fifteen then. I'd sneak out of the orphanage like a thief, praying no one would catch me."

"You weren't scared to walk the dark streets alone?"

"There are scarier things than dark streets out there. I always carried a pepper spray with me. I still use it."

Blossom Ford is a safe town, but occasionally, it has its creeps, just like most places everywhere.

"I wanted a quiet place to escape to. I've always been fascinated by the sun as well," she adds.

"Me too."

Still, "I'll pick you up, the days you want to come."

She's quiet, and I wonder if she feels I'm intruding too much in her life when our relationship is casual.

"Until you leave, or we call this thing off."

"What was it like, growing up at the orphanage?" I can't comment on her statement yet.

"I always thought I hated it. I always resented whoever my parents are for abandoning me; especially during the holidays or when I saw families having Sunday lunch at Jackson's diner. But after meeting others who grew up in state facilities while I was in college and during my internship there, I realized how lucky I was." She watches a duck swimming in the river.

"My carers didn't rape me or abuse me. Mrs. Gallagher, the orphanage manager, treated us like her own kids. She'd try to chat with us if she thought we were down. I think it helped that the orphanage is small and the folks of Blossom Ford are mostly generous."

"I think I understand a little why you don't like Christmas. Have you tried to find your parents?"

"Are you usually this chatty with your flings?"

"No. I've never shared my favorite spot in the world with any of them, either."

Aiyana is silent for a while.

"You're very good at making a girl feel special," she eventually says.

"Is it working?"

She shivers.

I shift behind her and embrace her. "It's warmer this way."

She relaxes and leans against my chest.

"I did, when I became an adult. I knew it was going to be difficult because I was left in the orphanage's front yard without a name or any identifying objects. That's why my surname is Ford. I hated it when kids made fun of me and the other kids for having the same surname. Anyway, when there was no way of finding them, I stopped looking back. I have a family anyway."

"Your found family."

"Isabella, Carmen, Mary Beth and Briana. We look out for each other and are present in each other's special moments."

I want to be someone Aiyana relies on.

"Is it strange to not be playing? I don't know what I'd do if I couldn't be a zoo vet."

I tuck my chin into her neck.

"The moment I realized I couldn't play, it was as if my life lost its purpose."

Aiyana draws circles on my arms.

"It's been hell."

I'm glad she says nothing because there's not much that can help.

"Are you going to take up one of the offers to coach?"

"You heard about that?"

"The sports news talks about it every day, it's hard not to. Some of the townsfolk are betting on which team you'll choose."

"I don't know what the hell I'm gonna do."

Apart from not letting her go.

"Why don't you date?" I ask.

Aiyana shrugs.

"I tried a few times. It didn't work."

"Maybe you dated the wrong guys."

"That's what Carmen said."

"She must have great intuition."

Aiyana shrugs again.

"Wanna have breakfast?" I ask.

"Sure, I'm off today. Tomorrow too. I'm not even on call, which is rare."

"We can eat at the diner."

"Hell no!" Aiyana pulls away and stands.

"What's the matter?"

"You're an international celebrity. In this town,

you're also a hero. You seriously think I'll rock up with you to the diner? We'll be the talk of the town for months to come. I like peace in my life. So no, thank you."

I can't help laughing. I want everyone to know she's mine so much I didn't think about how fast news flies in our small town.

"It's okay for you to laugh. You're used to the gossip. And you're probably leaving town. I live here permanently. There's no escape for me."

"Sorry."

"There was only one truck in the parking lot when I arrived. Is it yours?" Aiyana asks.

I nod, then get up and fold my blanket.

"I'll call and get something to go. They're used to me ordering double, because I save some for the next day. We can eat at my apartment."

There are more cars in the parking lot when we head over there. Aiyana is so careful about being seen with me, I have to stop myself laughing at the stealthy way she ducks into her car and drives off.

CHAPTER FIVE

Aiyana

WHEN I DROP by the diner, my order is ready. It's too early for the morning rush; there's hardly anyone inside.

"Watched the sunrise at The Point?" Rosie asks.

I still don't know how the townsfolk found out I watch the sunrise at the point. "Yes. Thanks Rosie, have a good day."

I take the food bags from her and hurry out before anyone comes in and stops me for a chat. I'm enjoying spending time with Finn and I'm ravenous.

I don't know if sharing important things about my life with him is a good thing or not, I'm just doing what feels good. Maybe it was watching the sunrise together, but I wanted to tell him about my life.

I'm going to enjoy this for as long as I can.

I park near him but go straight up. A few minutes later, he rings the bell.

"I tried to make it look like we're not together." He's wearing a cap, and a mask covers the bottom half of his face.

"You're enjoying this, aren't you?"

He laughs and takes his cap and mask off, places them on the coat rack in the hallway.

We sit opposite each other at the small table in the kitchen and dig into our eggs, bacon and sausages.

"I guess you're a pro at dealing with the press and the tabloids."

"It was part of my life. Whenever it got too much, I'd sneak into town, watch the sunrise and spend some time hiking in the mountains."

I watch the bracelet on his wrist as I drink the mocha I ordered. He slept with it. Now I think about it, he was wearing it at the engagement party. It was weird. He was wearing a state-of-the-art suit complete with bow tie, but on his wrist, there was this old bracelet that was clearly homemade. I'd seen it in photos of him, too.

"That bracelet is unique. You wear it like it's a part of you, but it doesn't seem like something you'd buy."

He asked personal questions, so I figure I can ask a few more of my own.

He's sips white coffee.

"My sister made it in fifth grade. It was my birthday present. It's almost thirty years old now. I think I may have to stop wearing it. It's been fixed so many times."

Isabella told me about his sister Fiona and how she'd passed in an accident when she was only ten.

"I didn't want to bring up painful memories."

Finn shakes his head. "When she left, I lived my life to the fullest, to enjoy every single day. I think that's what she'd have wanted for us."

He's always looked like he's doing that. Whether it's in the ice rink, partying with his teammates, being photographed with actresses and models, he's always looked like he was having a blast.

He stands and puts the paper plates, cups, and cutlery in the recycling bin.

I wipe the table, rinse the dishcloth in the sink.

Finn hugs me from behind.

"Done?"

I turn and face him.

"What do you have in mind?"

"Showing you my bedroom skills."

"I'm in."

He picks me up, my arms round his waist. It's good to be carried as if I weigh nothing. It makes me feel feminine.

In the bedroom, he undresses me slowly. Every time his hands brush against my bare skin, I shiver. Then he lays me down and forces me to watch him take his clothes off.

There's something sexy about watching each other. By the time Finn lies beside me, my breath comes in quick puffs.

He kisses every part of my face. Then nibbles my ear lobes and nips his way down my throat. I try to hurry him by pulling his head down to my breasts, but he wriggles out of my hands.

"Not yet."

I press my legs together, trying to ignore the need to be touched down there.

Finn looks at my jammed legs and smiles.

"Tease," I say.

"You'll enjoy it more, I promise."

He massages my breasts and the space between them, his eyes locked on the large mounds. I'm getting turned on by the way he's studying me!

When he finally inserts a nipple into his hot mouth, I scream in relief. He suckles on it sending arrows of pleasure to my core. Then he does the same to the other one.

My hips roll upwards, my legs spread of their own accord. I need release now. I stretch a hand towards my pussy. A few flicks will tip me over the edge.

"Not yet."

Finn stretches my arms above my head. His eyes dart around the room until they land on his clothes. He grabs his t-shirt and expertly ties my hands to the bed frame.

My breasts jut out and his gaze arrows there. I suck in a breath. Finn plays with my stomach, circles his tongue around my belly button. Then he moves to my legs and kisses the soft skin on the back.

"Finn,"

I'm watching his every move.

"Yes, Aiyana."

"Make me come."

He moves up to my thighs. Caresses the insides.

"See how wet you are? Your body is loving this. It'll be worth the wait."

He nibbles the soft skin. I didn't know my body was so sensitive. It's like every part of me has become an erogenous zone.

He stares at the v between my legs and licks his lips.

"I love how the caramel of your skins turns darker along the folds of your pussy."

With his tongue, he laps the juices in my slit, then licks my clit, up and down. I plant my legs on his shoulders and move against his mouth, keening now, desperate.

As if he knows I can't take anymore, Finn scissors me with his fingers and I come, screaming his name.

He shifts up my body and unties my hands.

"I'm going to fuck you slowly."

I'm so wet, he glides into me in one easy movement. I wrap my legs around his waist.

He strokes in and out of me leisurely. Simultaneously, he kisses me with long, unhurried thrusts against my tongue.

"Your wet pussy feels amazing against my bare cock."

I'm glad I told him I'm on the pill. I rake my hands down his back and squeeze his firm ass. He hardens inside of me, stretches me more.

I come up for air and bite his earlobe.

He sucks in a loud breath.

"Tease," he whispers.

"It'll be worth it."

"God, woman."

The strangled laughter in his voice makes me smile.

I tighten my pelvic muscles.

Suddenly, he's thrusting faster.

I reach between our bodies and squeeze his balls.

He groans and drives into me so hard the bed bangs against the wall.

I'm no longer laughing.

The pressure is building inside me again. Finn's powerful thrusts hit my sweet spot again and again.

We come apart at the same time.

"I can't move," he says when his body stops shuddering.

"Me too."

"Are you busy today? Can we stay in bed the whole day?"

I laugh. "You want to sleep the whole day?"

"What do you think?"

"I'm free."

CHAPTER SIX

Finn

IT'S SUNDAY AFTERNOON and I'm sitting in my truck, outside the place where my hockey career started. It's time to decide about my future. The offers I received are still good for another couple of weeks, but I want to commit to Aiyana. Let her know I want to make our casual relationship permanent.

To do that, I have to let her know what my life will be like. She's already averse to relationships. Plus, at forty-one, I'm sixteen years older than her. That's a hell of an age gap. Even though we're well matched in the bedroom and have a lot in common, she might prefer a younger man.

All my older brothers have younger wives and that doesn't seem to be a problem, but not all women are alike.

I always put one hundred percent in whatever I do. Winning Aiyana's heart will be no different. Sorting out my life is the first step.

With my cap and mask on, I enter the rink, my head down, and head for the last row. I spot coach straight away. He's more grizzled than the last time I saw him three years ago, but he's shouting at his kids to move, like he used to do when I was a teen.

Thirty years ago, Coach was brought in to bring the Blossom Ford High School Hockey team to its former glory days. I've loved hockey since I was little, but when I got into high school, Coach played a huge part in helping me realize a small town kid like me could make it to the National Hockey League.

I have many wonderful memories of playing and practicing here. The place has changed little. It's a small rink and has always felt homely to me. The festive decorations make it feel extra special.

I can tell without checking the scoreboard that Blossom Ford High School is losing. It's all there in Coach's posture and the home side parents' faces.

I spend the rest of the game checking out the players and their game. When everyone leaves at the end, I wander around the rink.

"Coach," I call out when the old man returns to the rink.

We greet each other, then sit.

"What do you think? It's not the National Hockey League, but the kids have a lot of heart and ambition.

They need the right man to guide them," Coach asks.

I think about my answer. Coach is retiring and asked if I'd consider taking over the team.

After I realized I couldn't play anymore, coach was the first person to bring up coaching, before offers from some of the most prestigious clubs in the game came in.

The low pay isn't an issue. Without responsibilities, I saved most of what I earned. Thanks to my brother Lorcan, who's a financial guru, that money continues to multiply.

What matters to me is loving what I do. I'm almost sure coaching a club in one of the big cities isn't for me. I'm not sure I could be a good teacher to the kids either.

"They need discipline," I say.

"You're already thinking like a coach. You're the right person for this job, Finn."

"What do I know about kids?"

"You were one, once. You know how they are feeling."

I think about that as I head home, after telling coach I'll make up my mind soon. No one is in when I arrive and I remember Mom, Dad and Aunt Caitlin are at some Church Christmas do. Our tree is up and is fully decorated with old ornaments and an angel at the top. Being home to help get it ready was great.

I switch on the festive lights outside, grab a beer and sit in one of the porch chairs.

A truck pulls up and parks beside mine. Rory climbs

out.

"Where's my sister-in-law?" I tease.

"Why? So you can pretend you're sick and ask her to help you?" He scowls.

"That was weeks ago."

Yet, I'm understanding why Rory wasn't pleased I tried to monopolize his wife's company the first time I met her, even though she only had eyes for him. I wouldn't want any man trying to take Aiyana's attention away from me, even if he were my brother.

I never thought of myself as possessive; I guess Aiyana brings that side of me out.

Rory sits beside me.

"Made up your mind about the offers coming in?"

I stare at the three houses around us and the land beyond. There's enough space for my brothers and I to each have a good-sized family home. Two of my brothers have already built theirs.

"I don't think I'll take any of the offers I got for the NHL clubs."

"You love this place too much."

I slug back some of my beer. There's no point offering Rory alcohol. He won't even have the allowed amount if he's driving.

"I guess I can play games all day."

Rory snorts.

"What about the High School team?" Rory asks.

"You mean coach them?"

"Why not? You know hockey inside out, you're

great with people. You always know how to bring out the best in them. And you can watch the sunrise and hike as much as you want."

I frown.

"They are high school kids. It's an important time. I've lived thinking mostly about myself for the last twenty years plus. It's an enormous responsibility."

"It is a tremendous responsibility. One you're more than qualified to take on. You were a team captain for nine years. And every one of those years, your team won the league. Most of your team are more than a decade younger than you and they respect you. That's not just because you're a great player. Coach saw that."

Rory gets up like he said his piece and enters the house.

"Are you here to pick up the pumpkin pie Mom made for your wife?" I shout at his back.

Rory doesn't reply. He comes out a little later with a wrapped plate and waves goodbye.

I'm thinking about our conversation when a little girl turns the corner of the house running, narrowly missing an inflatable reindeer. She freezes in front of me.

"Hi poppet," I smile at my seven-year-old niece. "Did you run away from Daddy?"

She remains silent but comes up to me. I scoop her onto my knee. Her scrunchy is about to fall away from her ponytail.

"Daddy is still learning to do hair," I say as I gently

remove the tie and redo the ponytail.

My niece has gone through so much, losing her mom the way she did. And yet, every day she's finding the courage to adapt to a new family and home.

I want to coach the high school team. I'm just afraid of letting the kids down, I realize. For so long, living my life to the fullest has meant being the best hockey player, partying whenever I could, loving women and spending time with family at home. Now I've found Aiyana and can no longer play hockey, some of my priorities have changed.

I am going to give my all to make sure I don't disappoint the kids. And I'll be living in the best town in the world, doing everything to make the woman of my life happy.

My brother Fallon rounds the corner of the house and climbs the porch steps. He stares at his daughter, who's still sitting on my lap. She faces the other direction, and Fallon sighs.

"News is all over town you took the job at one of the hockey clubs in Chicago and start next week," he says.

"What?"

"Apparently, it's in one tabloid."

Just in time, I remember the kid and stop myself swearing a blue streak. Damn paparazzi. What if Aiyana heard that rumor? I don't want her thinking I made the decision to leave town so soon without mentioning anything to her.

"Poppet, Uncle Finn has to go out," I say to the little

girl and pat her hair.

She scoots off my lap and scampers indoors.

Fallon watches her go.

I pat his shoulder. Maybe the joyful and giving spirit of Christmas will help our little girl heal. As I leave the house, I hope some of that magic will work on my relationship with Aiyana. Because right now, I'm about to play the biggest game of my life.

CHAPTER SEVEN

Aiyana

I END MY phone conversation with Carmen and place the cell phone beside me on the sofa. I don't know why I'm in a daze after hearing Finn is leaving town. He was going to leave, anyway.

I sigh. Hanging out with him is fun, and the sex is out of this world. He's funnier and more easygoing than I thought he'd be. I still can't believe I shared bits of my life I rarely talk about. He's actually a fan of my favorite nature program; we watched it most of yesterday afternoon. I hoped we'd have more time.

And I'm a little hurt, even though I've no reason to be.

When he left last night, he said he had something to do today. It must have been signing the contract for his new job. Being in a fling as we are, there's no need for him to tell me about something like this. It's my mistake to think what we shared yesterday was special; that even though we might go our separate ways, we'd formed some kind of special friendship.

Yesterday, he didn't seem to know what he was going to do. When did he decide to take up the job?

I remove the laundry out of the dryer and start folding. When I shake out a sheet with more force than I need to, I stop. I'm more than a little hurt.

I'm mad at myself too. The fact I'm so disappointed in Finn means I started expecting things from him. And that makes little sense, considering we spent less than forty-eight hours together.

I finish the laundry. It's only six in the evening and I already cleaned the house. I usually drag the chores; I don't like them and I'm so busy at the zoo that when I get free time, all I want to do is sleep. Since Finn was going to stop by more often, for the foreseeable future at least, I breezed through them.

I switch on the TV, grab an ice-cold beer and put on the nature channel. Then switch it off. It reminds me of how he wrapped the quilt around me and carried me in here to watch the show together. I'd unwrapped myself laughingly, and we'd both huddled in the quilt, eating microwaved popcorn.

The entire house reminds me of him. I need to get out and think, put him firmly in the didn't work out drawer of my mind. With a note: flings are not for me.

I head for the bedroom to put on my walking boots when the doorbell rings. It's Finn. I let him in, wondering what he's come to say.

"I'm about to go out."

He stares at me, then pushes in.

"You heard the rumors. Can we talk? Just for a little while," he says from the living room.

I sit on the chair near the couch.

"I've taken a job. In town, coaching the high school team."

"That's not what I heard. Which town?" I'm confused.

"What did you hear exactly?"

"You're leaving town to start a job next week."

"That's a rumor. I don't even know who started it. I'm getting a press conference organized in a couple of days to announce my new position."

I shake my head.

"I'm staying in Blossom Ford as the new high school coach. I confirmed it on my way to you."

I'm so shocked, I take a while to think of what to say.

"Why?"

"You don't think it's a job worth doing?"

"What?"

I stand and pace the small amount of free space in the room. "It's not that. I just never imagined such a high-profile player like you would give up the chance to coach a big team."

"You gave up better paid jobs to work at the zoo here."

I run my fingers through my locs. My mind was prepared for Finn to tell me he's living. This is a turn of events I didn't expect.

There's no reason for him to lie to me. The truth will come out soon. Besides, I believe him. I return to my seat. There's a serious expression on his face. Is he disappointed in me? I don't know what to think.

"I'm sorry I jumped to conclusions before talking to you. I know what this town's like and should have known better."

What I did was unlike me. Carmen warned me it was a rumor. She wasn't even going to tell me. It sort of slipped out.

"I won't be in the limelight like I used to, but if you hear any rumors about me in the future, promise you won't pay them any notice until you've talked to me."

Finn sounds so earnest that I promise him, although I don't see the need. How much longer can our casual relationship last?

He shifts onto the floor and sits cross-legged in front of me.

My heart races.

"Aiyana, yesterday at the river, I realized I'm in love with you."

A lump forms in my throat. His sea-green eyes suck me in and I believe him.

"I think it started before, when I met you. We hardly talked, but I was curious about you. I thought about you and now and then I'd ask Isabella about her friends so I could hear news of you."

He places his hands on my lap. "We agreed on a fling. I know you don't want a relationship. But please reconsider. We have so much in common, I truly believe we'll be happy together. I want to spend every day of my life making you happy because I love seeing you laugh."

"Finn."

I stop and swallow.

I'm terrified. Of things not working out again.

It feels different this time. I never clicked with any of my boyfriends the way I do with Finn. But, each time I started a new relationship, didn't I hope it'd be different? What if this ends out the same way, with Finn leaving?

"I love spending time with you. I Truly do."

I blink because my eyes are watering. I don't want our relationship to end.

"Then what's the matter, lass?"

The gentleness in his voice gives me courage.

"I love how you're gentle and strong and funny. You just seem to know how to love me."

He's quiet for a while. "I'm hearing you're

falling in love with me."

"I believe I'm starting to." It's the only thing that explains why I shared so much with him and was disappointed when I thought he'd lied to me about not knowing what he was going to do in the future. It also explains why I abandoned all sense and believed in a rumor. I wasn't thinking straight because I've started to develop feelings for him.

"Still, I'm scared this won't work out. I think the fact I was abandoned left a scar on me. It seems I push people away or I'm so afraid they'll leave one day, I never fully give my heart away."

"In my forty-one years, you're the only woman I've ever wanted to marry. I've met no one who made me this happy. I'm not going anywhere, I'll spend the rest of my life proving that to you, being your family."

I can't look away from him.

"Will you give me the chance, lass?"

CHAPTER EIGHT

Finn

MY HEART IS pounding. It should be enough that Aiyana found the courage to confide her fear in me. This is hard for her. I want more, though. I want her to trust me enough, to give me a chance to love her.

She nods.

I lay my head on her lap and wrap my arms around her lower back. She's undone me; I need a moment to blink away tears.

Aiyana pets my head.

I get up, hold her waist, and lift her. I can't help whooping with joy. Then I twirl.

She chuckles.

"The neighbors are going to complain."

"Once I explain, they'll be cheering for me."

Aiyana laughs again.

Then she showers my face with kisses.

"I want you," I say.

"So do I."

I keep her hugged to my chest and walk into the bedroom. We undress each other, then slip under the covers.

I cup her face. "Miss Aiyana Ford, thank you for finding the courage to trust me."

A tear slips down her face. I kiss it away.

"We're both crybabies," I whisper against her mouth and feel her lips curve upward.

I lift her arms above her head and intertwine our fingers. Her breasts mash against my chest. I kiss her slowly, savoring the intoxicating taste of her mouth.

"I love kissing you," she says when we come up for air.

"What about this?" I make a hickey on her throat.

She moans.

"I'll have to wear a high-necked top for work tomorrow."

"Don't. I want everyone to know you're no longer single. When is your next day off?"

"Tuesday."

I watch her warm brown eyes as I slide into her. They are dark with desire.

Her fingers tighten where they are joined with mine. Her lips part. She's so wet, I slide in and out of her in a smooth rhythm.

"Let's have lunch at the diner. I want everyone to

know you're mine, so no one dares to even look at you."

"What?"

I nip her bottom lip.

"On your next day off, let's eat at the diner."

"Hmmm."

I kiss her again. I want to make love to her for a long time, but the need to thrust into her fast is building.

Aiyana moans into my mouth. Her hips pick up speed. She's getting closer to the end, too.

The sensation of our skin touching all along the length of our bodies is amazing.

I ratchet up the pace, thrust deep into her and come fully out before driving back in.

"I love the way you match my every move, lass."

Her lids close.

I kiss them. She closes her eyes whenever she's close to coming.

"I love you," I say.

She screams my name as she orgasms, the contractions in her pussy squeezing my cock. A couple more pumps and I, too, find my release inside her welcoming body.

"I love you too," Aiyana says tentatively.

I shift. She moves with me until we're both lying on our sides, with my arms round her and her back against my chest. I can sleep in any position. I learned yesterday she sleeps better on her side.

I kiss her shoulder.

The way she said those three words is branded in my

mind. I can't wait for the day she can say them in a confident tone.

Although I've never been in love before, I know a lot about it from seeing Mom and Dad, Aunt Caitlin and Uncle Brian. I want my relationship with Aiyana to be like theirs. Loving, strong, and everlasting.

Love is a lot like a game. I have my trump cards–my bedroom skills, the things we have in common, the gift of my family - and I'll use them shamelessly whenever I think they'll make her happy.

EPILOGUE

Aiyana

Three Years Later

I PAT THE cranky old monkey and smile as he turns his head away. He's always grumpy when he's ill.

"This will make you feel better, I promise."

I give him a shot of the antibiotics he needs and watch as his keeper leads him out of the treatment room. I'm leaving the zoo late again. And it's Christmas Eve.

On my way home, almost every house is decorated with Christmas inflatables and lights. Instead of the mild dislike I used to feel before, there's a rush of anticipation. Just knowing I'm going to be going to church with all my family makes me hum. It boggles the mind how the sense of security from knowing I belong changes the way I view the holidays.

I slow down as the sign for O'Connor Premium Farm comes up. It's home. I drive up to our brightly lit house and park beside Finn's truck.

He comes out and opens my car door.

"No touching." I put my hand out to keep him away and clamber out of the car, the way only an eight-month pregnant woman would.

His expression makes me want to laugh, but I hold it back. It took him a while to get used to my rule of waiting until after I shower when I return from work, before we can have any contact. However, he finds it really hard to keep to that rule when he sees me struggling out of the car.

I shower as quickly as I can.

"Don't rush, we're not late."

"We'll be cutting it close, though."

"Everyone will understand. How was work?"

Finn helps dry my back and feet.

"Very busy. Old Charley is ill again. He was grumpy all day."

"I bet he loved seeing you three times a day. He's in love with you."

I giggle. "You think all men are in love with me."

"That's because you're beautiful, Mrs. Finn O'Connor."

He slides thick socks and flat boots on my feet as I fix my hair.

"How was your day?"

He makes a face.

"What happened?"

"Working from home is so hard! I have so many

plans and ideas to finalize for next season, yet I barely had time to sit down. First Fallon needed help to fix something for his little princess, then Dad had a Santa emergency."

I laugh so hard listening to everything that happened, tears stream down my face and ruin my makeup.

Every day, I'm grateful Finn and I have jobs we love. He's a brilliant coach.

I love being pregnant much more than I thought I would, but the back pain and the fact it takes me three times my usual amount of time to put shoes on is a dampener. I can't wait to give birth and welcome our little boy into the world and our home.

As I go down the stairs, I smooth my hand over the polished wooden banister. I'm so proud of the house Finn, my brothers- and father-in-law, built for us. Finn and I had so much fun going on trips to select the furnishings.

We've been married a year now, and every day I'm thankful I found the courage to trust him, because he's the best thing that happened to me.

"Do you have the presents?"

Finn points to two large bags.

"How are you going to sneak them in?"

I've been more tired than expected, but wanted to choose every present for our family with Finn, so they are only ready now. As far as I know, everyone else has placed their gifts under the tree at Big house number one. That's what I call Finn's parents' house. We're all meeting there before heading to church.

It isn't so much the adults I'm worried about, it's the kids. I don't want to spoil the innocence of Christmas for them.

"Best thing is, wait until everyone has left for church. We can join them later. Ready?"

We leave our beautiful house and stroll the short distance to Big house number one, the Christmas lights of the houses besides ours and the moon guiding our way.

The End

MARRYING THE PROTECTIVE PROFESSOR

CURVY BRIDES OF BLOSSOM FORD #1

August

ALL MY LIFE I've secretly wished I was born and raised in an ordinary family, with loving, welcoming parents instead of being the town's sign of bad luck, growing up at Blossom Ford Orphanage and having the town's name as my surname, like the other kids there. I can't help believing if I was wanted, the acceptance and sense of belonging would have helped me become someone who knows how to love. That belief is strongest when I think of Ella Mitchell.

It's Friday night so ensuring she gets home safely is my top priority as I park my SUV a short distance from Jackson's Diner where she's working, far enough to see the door of the restaurant but not so close that anyone might link my presence to the diner. I don't care how the interfering residents of Blossom Ford view me, but I don't want rumors to spread about Ella.

I slide down the car seat, getting comfortable even as I curse myself for the warmth that spreads through my chest at the mere thought of her name. As I've done a millionth time, I tell myself I'm here to protect her.

An uncomfortable tightness in my chest and a bitter taste in my mouth that I'm all too familiar with have me exhaling slowly. But it's hard to chase away the guilt. I cannot keep from committing the same sin. I'm a scarred, divorced, grizzly mountain of a man that's old enough to be her father while she's a beautiful, innocent twenty-two-year-old with her whole life ahead of her. Ella deserves better than me. But I still can't stop thinking about her.

It makes no difference that what I feel for her is more than physical attraction. I love her strength, soft smile and the way she's warm to everyone that crosses paths with her. There's a certainty in my bones that she's meant for me alone. This only makes the guilt worse. I should let her go because I love her.

And I have. To a point. For the last two years since I returned to Blossom Ford, saw her for the first time and fell for the kindness in her honey hued eyes and the sweetest curves I'd ever seen, I've stopped myself from approaching her. From claiming her. At least in real life. Because in my dreams, I've made love to her every single night and spent my days laughing with her. I've always considered my self-control one of my strongest attributes, but I can't stop dreaming about her.

I can't help the fact that I won't have her driving home by herself at midnight, after her shifts at the diner on Fridays and Saturdays. If I'm an asshole, so be it. And if deep down I know as well as ensuring she's safe, I have to see her face, I'll take the guilt and deal with it.

I frown when only two cars remain in the parking lot. One is old Jackson's beat up truck, and the other belongs to Rosie; the woman who works with Ella. Ella's old yellow mini should be right besides Rosie's.

The door to the diner flies open and Rosie marches out in her apron, phone glued to her ear. She sprints to her car. My frown thickens. How is Ella going to get home? Will she be closing on her own? I force myself to stay in the car. As much as I want to rush in and help, keeping a distance is crucial to my self-discipline.

I ramp up the air conditioning in the car a little higher. It usually takes one hour to close, but tonight, it'll take Ella longer. Old Jackson doesn't think hard work hurts women. There's no way he's going to help with setting the dinner to the way he likes it.

I keep my eyes on the door and an hour and a half later, I'm rewarded with the sight of Ella's curvy hips wrapped in hugging denim and the soft way her breasts hug her blouse. Even after a ten-hour shift, she's a vision that gets my heart racing.

She zeroes in on my car and it's like she can see me, like she knows I'm waiting here for her. She does this on Fridays and Saturdays; the days I wait for her. If she worked any other nights, I'd wait for her then, too. She's friends with Mrs. Gallagher, the orphanage director who's the closest thing to a mother I've ever had. Ella must think of me as a much older brother who's looking out for her.

She steps on the street and heads towards me. I know that she's just taking the road to her house, but I can't stop my heart from beating even faster. It's like this every time I see her.

I'm feeling something else too; anger. Her walking alone down the empty street at this time of the night is pissing me off.

She's only a few feet from me when a car careens down the street and stops beside her. I sit up straight, hoping a friend is coming to pick her up. But she doesn't slow down, even after spotting the car.

I scowl as a man stumbles out of the car and steps in her path. It's Toby Anderson, Ella's ex. Something ugly rears in me. Despite my unstoppable feelings for Ella, whenever I see him, I realize how great my self-control is. Every time I saw him with Ella, I wanted to knock him out. The four months they dated were an exercise in self-discipline I didn't think I was going to win. But for Ella, to give her the chance at happiness she deserved with someone her age that could give her a comfortable life, I held myself back.

I don't like the way Toby sways on his feet. The light from the full moon and lamppost in front of the diner are enough to make out the disgust on Ella's face.

Before I know it, my hand is on the door handle, but my eyes don't stray from Toby.

They are talking but the loud music and shouts from the car stop me from hearing what they are saying. Toby reaches out a hand and touches Ella's arm. She wrenches it back.

I'm out of the car. I sprint towards them, her safety the only thought in my mind. for her, I'd tried staying away, but her safety is something I'll not compromise on. even if it means she might hate me for interfering with her life.

FAKE MARRYING THE BODYGUARD

THE O'CONNORS OF BLOSSOM FORD #4

Bonnie

I KEEP MY eyes tightly shut and listen for noises around me. It's too quiet. I'm used to the sounds of cars honking, people going about the apartment. Then a sudden high sound startles me and I grab the bed sheet. I take a while to work out it's a bird call.

When my heart settles, I can tell I'm alone. I know the feeling of being watched all too well; this isn't it. I allow myself to open my eyes and stare around an unfamiliar, semi dark room. Instead of white stone walls and marble floors, there are wooden walls and floors.

My breath hitches when I notice the large window opposite me. The sun is setting and the deep orange and pink colors inside the golden ball are breathtaking. There are trees outside with some of their leaves turning a burnt orange; it's a mesmerizing depiction of fall. A little while later, I realize I'm still staring and pull myself up on it.

I don't know where I am, so why am I admiring the view? I'm usually so vigilant about my environment. Have I finally gone mad, like Dad always said I would one day?

I shake my head. I move the soft bed sheet aside and look down at my body, taking in the white dress.

Memories of Rory, the wedding and escaping the life I lived for twenty years return.

I must have fallen asleep on the way here. This must be his cabin.

A soft knock sounds. My eyes shift to the door. Heart pounding, I tumble out of the massive bed and stand. I try to answer, but no sound comes out of my mouth. I clear my throat and try again, using all my acting skills to strengthen my voice.

"Yes?" There's no sign of the nerves trying to strangle my throat. I hide my trembling hands behind my back.

"It's Rory. Can I open the door?"

Even if he hadn't identified himself, I would have known it was him. There was something unique about the lilting rhythm of his deep voice. It made me want to relax around him, want to trust him.

When I say yes, he opens the door but doesn't leg to of it. Light enters the room, allowing me to see the way his sea-green eyes rove over me before they return to my face. Some of the tension leaves me. His gaze is familiar, he's looked at me like that countless times in the year he's guarded me.

What's different is his attire. I've never seen him in anything other than a white shirt and dark suit. He's wearing a t-shirt that outlines his muscles and low hanging blue jeans. My heart skips a beat and this time it has nothing to do with nerves. His auburn hair is wet, as if he's just come out of a shower. He looks younger than his forty-one years. More approachable. I swallow, struggling with my unsuitable and unwanted attraction to this man, who just happens to be my husband.

"Dinner is ready. Come have a bite, lass."

Why does it feel like he's showering me with affection whenever he calls me by that word? I can feel my nose crinkle as I try to stare him down, to figure out why he used that word. He stares back blankly, then shuts the door, leaving me in semidarkness again.

I bring my hands in front of me. Even though my heart is still racing and my body feels alive, my fingers are steady. I'm attracted to but not scared of him.

Can I really trust Rory the way my body seems to believe it can? Or have I escaped from my controlling father only to fall into the hands of a more wicked monster?

I didn't always feel like I could trust Rory. Dad contracted his personal bodyguard services firm after the company he previously used failed to catch my stalker for three years. The stalker had become more dangerous, nearly kidnapped me once.

That's when Dad brought Rory in, even though he seemed to have reservations about hiring the ex-Mixed Martial Arts athlete. I'd never understood that. The Red King, as Rory was called by those in the sport, was Dad's favorite fighter. Now, maybe I do. He seems decent, somehow different from Dad.

The men that guarded me were also my jailors. I'd learned the hard way that all the workers in the house, no matter their position, were Dad's people. Rory terrified me the most. First, for the same reason Dad loved the MMA fighter. His explosive, merciless fighting style. It made me think he was cruel. The other reason was scarier. For the first time in seven years, I was behaving like a high school girl with a severe crush. I did my damnedest to hide my growing attraction.

But only three months later, his security team caught the stalker when he attempted to kidnap me again. Rory's powerful arms had held me against the strong column of his chest and stroked my damp hair.

"You're safe, lass," he'd said softly, emotion lacing his voice as if he really cared about me.

I told myself he was doing his job, that he was the type of competitive person who had to always win and the emotion in that ragged, comforting voice of his was pride. However, since then, it became almost impossible to hide my attraction. Worse, I'm developing feelings for him.

The way he interacted with me didn't change but I

began putting a different meaning to his cryptic once overs when he started a shift. I couldn't shake the feeling he was checking to see if I was alright.

After watching him for six months since the stalking incident, I worked up the courage to ask him for help. I had to escape from Dad. My life had become a survival game long ago, and I was exhausted from living that way. I sang and smiled for crowds, but I'd lost my passion for singing, the only thing that gave me joy for so long.

To the public, I was a bubbly singer with millions of fans, but my private life comprised long hours of practice, rigorous diets and exercises imposed by Dad. I had tried escaping once, only to be brought back by one of my so-called bodyguards. He controlled my fortune and made decisions about my welfare. My will to live was disappearing at the thought of having to live that way for the rest of my life.

One day, while I was out doing the exercises Dad insisted on, I pretended to fall. When Rory helped me up, I explained how Dad was blackmailing me with two videos he took of me thrashing his study when I was seventeen and twenty-one. He was threatening to have me put under a conservatorship. I have no memory of vandalizing his study, but it was me in those videos. I suspected Dad drugged me, but had no way of proving that.

I was ready to give him all my fortune if he could help me flee. If he will enter a temporary marriage contract with me, before Dad got wind of anything, it'd be extremely hard to impose a conservatorship when I had a spouse willing to testify my mental capacity was sound. Especially if it was someone as influential as Rory.

"What if I do the same thing your dad is doing? I could keep your money and control you the way he does," Rory had asked, sea-green eyes steady on mine, as he crouched beside me on the green grass of the park.

It was the start of summer and a hot day but I went ice cold. I'd searched his face, lack of trust in my ability to judge people strong. Since the age of five, I grew up with Dad telling me people couldn't be trusted, that they didn't care for me. The only thing they loved was my voice and the smiling singer Bonnie. Maybe I was wrong about Rory.

I'd strengthened my back, focused on his steady gaze.

"I won't carry on the way I am."

"Okay, lass. I'll draft the papers. The only way to make sure you're permanently safe is to get those files, anything else he might have, and find something on him to make him believe if he ever tries to control you again, he'll be ruined."

"Is that possible?" My heart was in my mouth.

"Nothing is impossible where humans are concerned."

It took Rory three months to get everything sorted. Three long months of hope and fear. Usually, Dad left me alone, trusting in the army of people he'd placed around me to report my daily life. We had lunch together once a month at his favorite restaurant. I thought he'd see something was up, that I'd mustered the courage to flee. When he suspected nothing, I was so thankful he'd forced me to take acting classes.

Rory and his team found out Dad was involved with an organized crime ring of underage prostitution. A friend of his married us before Rory threatened Dad with providing proof of his illegal activities to the police if he ever tried to force me back to him.

I switch on the bedside lamp and gaze around the room. My one suitcase and guitar are under the window. I remove a flowing maxi dress and run my fingers through the soft fabric. It's one of the few dresses I'd hidden from Dad.

No matter how much he controlled my diet and exercises, my chubbiness never went away. His solution, which never really worked, was to have me wear body-shaping outfits at home, too. For a while now, I have hoped to wear maxi dresses whenever I wanted.

I get clean underwear and toiletries. I'm a little fazed that there's no ensuite in the bedroom, but I shake it off. Compared to the fact I might live life my way, it's only a minute drawback.

Rory's standing by the sink when I open the door. I was quiet but he must have heard, because he turns around. He's wearing a white apron knitted with a large picture of one of the Sesame Street characters. It covers almost all the apron.

A chuckle comes out of me before I can stop myself.

"Something funny?" His face is impassive.

It only causes me to crack up again. I cover my mouth with my free hand, unsure of what to say. My eyes refuse to move away from the knitted character. It looks so alive.

"My Mom and Aunt Caitlin made this apron especially for me. It's one of my favorites."

"It's beautiful. I mean, it looks good on you."

His lips lift.

My hands tighten on my clothes. Because I've just gone from humor to heat in a heartbeat. My cheeks flush. I can't drag my eyes away from that sexy face of his. I've never seen Rory smile like this. Like he doesn't have a care in the world, like an innocent boy.

"Do you mean it?" He asks.

"Mean what?"

"This overall looks good on me."

Did his eyes darken? He's no longer smiling, but I'm not exactly worried. Something about the way he's watching me is putting my body on alert. A panty melting kind of alert.

"Where's the bathroom?" I ask, unsure of what the tension between us means.

He points to a closed door and I dash in, locking the door. I wash and dress slowly, going over our conversation again and again, but I can't work out the meaning behind the expression in his eyes.

I give myself a stern lecture before I exit the bathroom. I've just left one prison. My body may feel Rory is safe, but I don't know him well.

Right now, Dad is petrified of what Rory might do, so sticking to him gives me the best protection against being dragged back to my old life. However, still I have to be careful of Rory and any people I meet.

Even if Rory has no evil intentions towards me, I still must keep myself from falling further for him. No matter how much I wish he were truly in love with me and wanted to spend the rest of his life with me, it's not likely to happen. What could a successful, ruggedly handsome man in his prime like Rory, want with an insecure, inexperienced, chubby woman like me, when he has the world's most beautiful women vying for his attention?

OTHER BOOKS BY THE AUTHOR

CURVY BRIDES OF BLOSSOM FORD SERIES

MARRYING THE PROTECTIVE PROFESSOR

MARRYING THE GRUMPY DIRECTOR

MARRYING THE POSSESSIVE NEIGHBOR

MARRYING THE WIDOWED DOCTOR

MARRYING THE SCARRED SOLDIER

MARRYING THE OBSESSIVE CEO

MARRYING THE BIG MOUNTAIN MAN

THE O'CONNORS OF BLOSSOM FORD SERIES

MATCHED TO PATRICK

REDEEMING THE MOUNTAIN MAN

BROTHER'S BEST FRIEND OBSESSION

FAKE MARRYING THE BODYGUARD

ABOUT THE AUTHOR

Iris West writes short and spicy romance about alpha heroes and the women they can't help falling in love with. She loves reading all types of romance books that have a happy ending and is an avid Kdrama fan.

Follow or like her on Facebook, Instagram Tik Tok and/or Goodreads.

FREE BOOK

Would you like a free book? Sign up to my mailing list at https://dl.bookfunnel.com/t191w45ryj to receive a copy of Loving My Fake Husband, a Curvy Brides of Blossom Ford short story.

HELP OTHERS FIND THIS BOOK

Thank you for reading A Fling For Christmas. If you enjoyed this book, please help others discover it by leaving a review at your favorite online bookstore.

Many thanks,

Iris xx